Marvella
TAKES
Flight

ANNETTE DANIELS TAYLOR

ILLUSTRATED BY KATHIE WATT

An imprint of Enslow Publishing

WEST **44** BOOKS™

MARVELLA FINDS HER MAGIC

MARVELLA IS A MODEL!

MARVELLA TAKES FLIGHT

Please visit our website, www.west44books.com.
For a free color catalog of all our high-quality books,
call toll free 1-800-398-2504.

Cataloging-in-Publication Data
Names: Daniels Taylor, Annette.
Title: Marvella takes flight / Annette Daniels Taylor.
Description: New York : West 44, 2023. | Series: The marvelous Marvella J.Q.
Identifiers: ISBN 9781538384503 (pbk.) | ISBN 9781538384497 (library
bound) | ISBN 9781538384510 (ebook)
Subjects: LCSH: Endangered species--Juvenile fiction. | Biodiversity
conservation--Juvenile literature. | Witches--Juvenile fiction.
Classification: LCC PZ7.D365 Ma 2023 | DDC [F]--dc23

First Edition

Published in 2023 by
Enslow Publishing
2544 Clinton Street
Buffalo, New York, NY 14224

Editor: Caitie McAneney
Illustrator: Kathie Watt
Cover Design: Leslie Taylor

Printed in the United States of America

CPSIA compliance information: Batch #CW23W44: For further information contact
Enslow Publishing LLC at 1-800-398-2504.

The Marvelous Marvella J. Q.

Meet Marvella

Name:
MARVELLA JUANITA QUINCY

Age:
8 AND A HALF!

From:
BORN IN BROOKLYN, BASED IN BUFFALO.

Favorite Animals:
CATS, OF COURSE.

Likes:
SUNGLASSES, CUPCAKES, RHINESTONES,
AND ALL ANIMALS.

Dislikes:
DIVORCE, MOVING, AND BIG MEAN BULLIES.

Biggest Secret:
DON'T TELL ANYONE, BUT ...
I CAN TALK TO ANIMALS!

Dedicated to Timmy A Michael.
Thank you for sharing El Yunque!

CHAPTER ONE

Vacation Vibes

Three weeks. Three weeks and I'll be lying on the beach in Puerto Rico, fresh juice in one hand. Glittery glam sunglasses on my face. No school for a whole week! Just sun, fun, and family.

"Marvella," Ms. Berry snaps. "What are you daydreaming about?"

Oh no! I'm caught. Was I drooling? I look away from the window in my classroom. I look to the class hamster, who gives me a thumbs up. Okay, no drooling. Phew!

Dad says it's always best to be honest. And even though I don't live with him since the divorce, I still try to do as he taught me. So I tell

Ms. Berry, "Well, I'm thinking about Christmas break. Mom, Tía Marisol, and I are going to Puerto Rico to visit my family!"

"You're from Puerto Rico?" my friend Rocco says, like it never occurred to him.

"On my mom's side," I say proudly.

Ms. Berry says, "Well, then you'll be interested in our lesson today, if you *pay attention.*"

"I'm all ears now, Ms. Berry!" I promise.

"We're learning about endangered animals and their ecosystems," says Ms. Berry. "One ecosystem with endangered animals is a tropical forest. And we only have one tropical forest in our national forest system—El Yunque. It's in Puerto Rico!"

Now I'm interested! Ms. Berry pulls up a video on her interactive white board. Summer heat. Bright sun. Green leaves and palm trees. So many kinds of green! I'm so ready for my vacation.

Ms. Berry continues. "El Yunque is very biologically diverse." She looks around the classroom. Her eyes land on one of my best friends, Autumn. "Who knows what *biologically diverse* means?"

Autumn's hand shoots up. "Biologically diverse means it's home to many different kinds of animals and plants!"

"That's correct!" Ms. Berry announces.

"In other words, El Yunque has biodiversity!" Autumn adds, reminding us how smart she is. I love that she knows something about everything! Dad says it's good to have friends you can learn something from.

All of a suddenly, my hand is raising.

"Yes, Marvella?" Ms. Berry asks.

"My *abuelita* lives in Puerto Rico," I say. *Abuelita* is Spanish for *grandma*. "I bet she'll take me to El Yunque if I ask her!"

Ms. Berry claps her hands together. "That's great! You can write a special report about El Yunque for extra credit while you're there. We'll learn so much from you."

"Uh," I begin. "But—"

"We'll talk before winter break," Ms. Berry says, cheerfully.

Great. Now I have homework for the holidays!

I walk home from the bus stop with Autumn and Rocco. Marigold Street in Buffalo, New York, is super different from Eastern Parkway in Brooklyn, New York. That's where

I used to live. There are tons of things I miss about my old life, but I love living next to my friends now. Plus, all the neighborhood animals know me.

That's because I have special Speller powers. I can talk to animals! I know the rooster who wakes me up every morning, the mice that live in Tía Marisol's super-old house, and every bird in the old oak trees! "Hi, Marvella!" says a big black crow. All Rocco and Autumn hear is *caw, caw*!

I wave at him, then stomp through some crunchy red and yellow leaves. I'm still mad about that extra homework!

"You know, Marvella, it's probably not *mandatory*," Autumn says. "That means you don't *have* to do it. You only have to do it if you want the extra credit."

Rocco wrinkles his nose. "Who wants to do homework if you don't have to?"

"Are you really going to Puerto Rico for Christmas?" Autumn asks.

"Yup!" I say.

"Aren't you going to miss the snow?" Autumn asks. "It's supposed to snow by Christmas!"

"Miss the snow?!" Rocco shouts. "Who

misses snow when they're swimming in the *ocean*?!"

"I love snowy winter holidays in Buffalo!" Autumn says.

I say, "Christmas in Puerto Rico is special to me. I haven't been there in a couple years, but we have special traditions. San Juan Airport's holiday lights are *ah-may-zing*. People cover palm trees in ornaments and lights. My favorite part is watching Santa water ski at the beach. He tosses candy and toys onto the sand!"

Now that I might not *have* to write that report, I'm getting excited about vacation again!

CHAPTER TWO

Raining On My Daydreams

"Welcome home, Marvellita!" Tía Marisol calls out as I walk in the door. A plant called a golden pothos sits in the foyer. Its green leaves have yellow streaks. It climbs in its clay pot. It reaches toward the light that streams in from the stained glass window by the stairs. Tía Marisol's house is filled with plants. She's a plant scientist, with her own lab and everything. Plus, growing plants is her special Speller power!

"Wash your hands," Tía continues. "I'm in the kitchen."

Tía Marisol cuts vegetables for dinner.

The TV is on. Tía is watching a weather report.

Tía kisses my cheek. "Did you have a good day, Marvellita?"

I shrug. "Yeah, I guess. But I told Ms. Berry about Christmas in Puerto Rico. Now, I hafta write a report during vacation!" I start daydreaming about sitting on the beach again. Living my best life.

Tía Marisol makes a concerned face. But it's not about what I just told her. It's about something on the TV. "They're predicting a bad hurricane."

"In Puerto Rico?" I ask. This cannot be happening. We're just about to *go* there! "But aren't weather people wrong a lot?"

Tía Marisol smiles. "Sometimes. But I know this meteorologist. She's my friend. Her name is Dr. Angela Navarro. She's one of the best in the country. If she says a big hurricane is coming—it's coming."

All of a suddenly, I'm not only thinking about my vacation. "What about Abuelita?" I ask. "Is she okay?"

Tía says, "The wind is already pretty bad. It's making it hard to put a call through."

Tía looks at me. Like she can read my mind, like Mom. She sees that I'm scared. "We'll call again later. Promise."

I sit up in my room, trying to focus on homework. Ms. Berry's making us do a bunch of reading about different kinds of ecosystems, or places animals live. Normally, anything about animals is my jam. But I can't concentrate. Not with Abuelita in the path of a hurricane!

I wish my Speller power was controlling the weather. But there's not much I can do about a hurricane. Then I get an idea. I can ask Mama Sparrow. Her nest is right outside my window.

"Mama Sparrow," I say. "You hear from all the birds migrating south for the winter. Have any of them talked about a hurricane?"

"Marvella," Mama Sparrow sings sadly. "Oh, yes. Lots of hurricane talk today! But lucky for us, it's very far from here. It'll hit a tropical place called the Caribbean. Do you know where that is?"

"Puerto Rico is in the Caribbean!" I gasp. "If the scientist says it's true and the birds say it's true, then this hurricane is for *real*."

"Marvella!" A voice calls my name.

"That's my mom," I explain to Mama Sparrow. "Thanks for the info." She flies off to find some food.

"One minute, Mom!" I yell.

"Abuelita got through!" Mom yells. I drop my school book and run to her.

CHAPTER THREE

Abuelita's Powers

Abuelita is video chatting with Mom and Tía Marisol. I've never been so happy to see her face on that phone screen! She looks a lot like Tía Marisol, except her hair is all gray, with four cornrows reaching down her back. Her deep, dark brown eyes look like Mom's. Her green work vest makes her look like an explorer.

Abuelita isn't like a little old lady grandma on TV. She hikes in the forest and climbs mountains on the regular. Inside Abuelita's house looks like the outside—full of tropical plants.

"Princesa Marvellita!" Abuelita says when she sees me. I like when she calls me *princess*!

"Hi, Abuelita!" I say, with a wave.

Behind Abuelita, I see big glass sliding doors. Trees and plants blow around in the background.

"Ai, *Mami*," Mom says. "Board your windows up! For protection against the winds."

"Maritza and Miguel are doing that," Abuelita answers. They are my aunt and uncle.

"Mami," Tía Marisol says seriously, "Hurricane Harley may change Christmas."

Abuelita looks sad. "Yes, I know, *mija*. This hurricane is going to be different—I can feel it. This one will be bad. I'll miss our visit. But right now, I'm more concerned with the Boriquen parrot's safety."

"What's a bor-EE-kwen parrot?" I ask. That's a hard word to say!

"*Mijas!*" Abuelita says, yelling at her daughters. "Don't you tell Marvella about her heritage?! Her roots?"

Tía and Mom look at each other. Then at Abuelita. "We will!" Mom says. "We *just* got her used to the idea she's a Speller. We'll cover family heritage soon, Mami. I promise."

"Ladies!" I shout because no one ever answers my questions. "What's a Boriquen parrot?!"

Abuelita begins. "We've lost many parrots here, *mijita*. Boriquen parrots are the last parrots born on our island. Once there were thousands of green, blue, and red feathered friends living in the forest. Today less than fifty are left among the Boriqua."

"Bor-EE-kwa?" I repeat after her. Abuelita nods. "What's Boriqua?"

"*Mijas!*" Abuelita says, scolding Mom and Tía Marisol. This is fun to watch! "You are Boriqua. We are from Boriquen. That's the

13

name of our home. When the Spanish came here, they renamed it *Puerto Rico*. But we're always Boriqua. Taíno Indian people. Mixed with Spanish. Mixed with West African people who were brought here to be slaves. All three groups became family. Today we are Boriqua!"

"Wow!" I say, imagining all those people living together and blending into one community. "We have a big family!"

Abuelita nods. Then her face freezes on the screen.

"We're losing the signal," Mom says.

"The wind is—" says Abuelita, her voice going in and out. "—picking up! Might ... lose service." Abuelita says to Mom and Tía Marisol, "Promise me you'll tell Marvellita our story."

Then she cuts out.

CHAPTER FOUR

Feathered Friends In Danger

I'm sitting in my room that night, hugging my knees. I'm so worried about Abuelita. And those Boriquen parrots! She seemed really worried about them.

Mom and Tía Marisol come in to say goodnight. "Marvellita, you look nervous," Mom says.

"Well, Abuelita is in the path of the biggest storm *ever*, and there are apparently parrots in danger, too! We're learning about endangered animals in Ms. Berry's class. They could *die out*. Like, there'd be no more left!"

My powers make me feel for every animal—no matter how small or far away.

Tía says, "In Puerto Rico, parrots have been endangered for decades."

"Why?" I ask.

"Poachers mostly," Mom answers. "Those are people who take parrots against the law. Today many are taken as pets. In the past, it was for their feathers."

"Their feathers?" I say. "That's just wrong!" I know a thing or two about nature-friendly fashion ever since my dad became top-fashion-designer Kendra Adams's photographer. Everyone has the right to be glam. But only if it's not hurting anyone!

"Habitat loss is another big problem for parrots. People cut down trees to build. But hurricanes can harm habitats, too." Tía continues, "But there's more. Get some sleep now, and I'll tell you tomorrow."

Tía Marisol promised she'd give me the full story after school. So, of course, I didn't sleep at *all*. A kid needs her beauty rest! I throw on a pair of Kendra Adams eco-friendly sunglasses and head to school.

"We talked about El Yunque yesterday," Ms. Berry begins. "So it's a good time to talk about Puerto Rico and Hurricane Harley."

I feel my heart sink all the way into my feet. There's no escaping this topic! I almost wish I could go back to daydreaming out the window.

"Ms. Berry," I blurt out. "We're not going to Puerto Rico anymore. Because of Hurricane Harley."

"That's too bad, Marvella," Ms. Berry says. "Hurricane Harley is still damaging the island. We're organizing a fundraiser for people hurt by the hurricane."

"And the animals?" I ask. "Some are endangered, right?"

Ms. Berry nods. "Sea turtles, snakes, birds—"

All of a suddenly, I feel like my head is spinning with questions and worries. "But like what even *is* a hurricane? Can it kill *all* the parrots?"

Ms. Berry pulls up a video of a hurricane online. Trees are bending! Houses are being ruined!

"Hurricanes are tropical storms," Ms. Berry explains. "It's called a hurricane if the wind speed and strength is bad enough. Hurricanes can destroy trees which parrots use for their homes. Parrots don't make their nests like lots of other birds. They look for ready-made homes—trees with holes dug out from other birds or bugs."

"Why can't they go to another tree or make another nest?" Rocco asks.

"Puerto Rican parrots only want certain trees. If those trees are damaged, they have nowhere to live and grow families."

"That's bad news, Ms. Berry," I say, shaking my head.

"You know what, I have an idea," says Ms. Berry. "Now that you're no longer going to Puerto Rico, you don't have to write that report about it."

Yes! I think. Something good could come out of this mess at least.

Score! Rocco mouths my way.

"Instead," says Ms. Berry, "*everyone* in class can write a report about one animal that is endangered and how it might be affected by habitat loss. Then look up ways to help save it!"

"Aw, man!"

"Urgh!"

"Marvella!"

My classmates are *not* happy with me.

"The report will be due after winter break," says Ms. Berry. "You'll have plenty of time to look up facts and write your reports!"

Holy abracadabra! It's not like I made Ms. Berry give all of us winter break homework. Right?

"Thanks, Marvella, for planting the report idea in my mind!" Ms. Berry says.

Just like that, she kills my social life with one sentence.

CHAPTER FIVE

Answers In The Attic

The second I get home from school, I throw open the front door and yell, "Tía Marisol, I need answers, *now!*" No answer. I check every room. Then, at the top of the stairs, I hear someone walking around above me.

"Come on up, Marvellita!" Tía Marisol calls from the attic. We *never* go in the attic. "Watch your step. The stairs are creaky. Two hundred years old."

I climb up the old stairs. The afternoon sun streams through a window. I haven't been in the attic before. It's a little dark and dusty. Boxes, crates, and old furniture live up here with dust balls. In the corner of my eye, I see something dart by.

Tip and Tap. My two mice friends are running around getting ready for their dinner.

Tip argues with Tap about breadcrumbs. "Cut it out, guys. I'll get you more breadcrumbs later. This is *important*," I say.

Tía Marisol looks up. She's looking through a big box. She removes a photo in a silver frame.

Tip and Tap slip under a door.

"What's behind that door?" I ask Tía Marisol.

Tía Marisol laughs, "You ask so many questions."

My curiosity is on high alert. "You said good scientists ask questions!"

She shakes her head. "You're right about that, Marvellita."

"Tía," I say, "there isn't a doorknob on the door. How do we get inside?"

"We don't," she answers.

Well, I decide to peek. But there's no keyhole to look through. Tía Marisol giggles at me and shakes her head. So, I get on the floor and try to look under the door. Tip and Tap ran in, so there's *something* behind the door.

"Okay," I say. "I give up. I can't see anything!"

"Probably because," Tia pauses and gives a look, "it's none of your business."

I cross my arms and pout. "Come here," she says, holding the silver frame.

"This is your great-great-*great* abuela, Ophelia Marisol Manzana," Tía Marisol says. "You have the same smile."

Looking at the photograph, I see a parrot is sitting on Abuela Ophelia's shoulder. She's also holding a tiny frog in the palm of her hand. Her hair is worn in two long cornrows held with a bow on each braid. Her dress has lace on the collar and sleeves. The photo is old. Black and white. Abuela Ophelia is surrounded by trees.

"That's a Boriquen parrot?" I ask.

"Yes," Tía answers, "and a coquí. That little frog."

"Why is Abuela Ophelia so special?" I ask.

"She was the first in our family to have her wish granted on the Spell Star," Tía answers. Tía's fingers point toward the window, as if Puerto Rico were right outside. "Ophelia wished to know the forest."

"What's that mean?" I ask. "To know the forest? How do you know the forest? Like, the trees and the animals, or the mountains and dirt?"

"Exactly, Marvellita! All of those things,"

22

Tía says. "Let me tell you a story. One evening Ophelia cannot sleep. She sits outside her balcony watching the stars. She sees a star falling and makes her wish. That night she has a dream. She knows that if she can find the star, her wish will be granted."

"How could she find the star?" I ask.

"Stars are in outer space. Like, they can't land anywhere on Earth!"

"That's usually true," Tía answers. "But we're talking about magic, Marvellita."

Tía continues the story. Tip and Tap run out from under the secret door.

"Far up the mountains of El Yunque, Ophelia discovers the star. It leaves a big crater on one of the mountain peaks."

"What'd the star look like? Glittery? Or was it just a big old rock?" I ask. I would *love* a glittery rock! It would match my glittery sunglasses. Ooh, and my glittery shoes …

"At first it does look like an old rock," Tía answers. "But after she touches it, it changes. It shakes and breaks. The old rock cracks and splits. Light rushes out of it! Suddenly, the most beautiful bird flies from the rock."

"A bird?" I whisper, totally into this story.

"Not just any bird, Marvellita," Tía says. "A magical Boriquen parrot!"

"This parrot gives Ophelia her wish to know the forest," Tía Marisol says. "A power that will be passed to her children, and their children, and their children."

"So, knowing the forest is like making plants grow?" I ask.

"Listening to the wind. Feeling how the

animals and people feel. Talking to the earth," Tía Marisol says. "The enchanted Boriquen parrot taught Ophelia to listen. And she learned."

"That's so cool," I say. But then I think about different fairytales I've read.

"What's the catch?" I ask.

"Huh?" Tía asks.

"What did the parrot want in exchange?" I ask. "Every fairytale I ever read has a catch. A way you can get tricked or lose your treasure."

"Ah, the catch. Well, Ophelia knew it was then her responsibility to protect the Boriquen parrot," Tía says. "She was its caretaker. She must always use her powers to help. And then her family after her."

"That's us," I say. Tía nods. "So what happens if this hurricane wipes out all the Boriquen parrots?"

Tía frowns and looks away. "We lose our magic."

CHAPTER SIX

Too Much For Morning

Saturday mornings are for sleeping late. But Mr. Rooster doesn't understand this. His morning announcements that the sun is up get on my nerves! He lives on the next block over. I shout out my window for him to quiet down.

Mr. Rooster crows back, "Miss Marvella, joy in the sun cannot be silenced!" I roll my eyes.

My cats take over my *whole* bed. Pudding cuddles at my feet and Velvet sleeps on my head. But Mr. Rooster's song gets my furry BFF's out of my bedroom. Morning means breakfast time—their favorite.

Then they're back. Pudding's on my bed, batting at my nose. Velvet jumps up onto the bed, too. Staring me down.

"What?" I moan.

"Mee-row—hungry!" Pudding says.

"Really?" I whine. "My eyes aren't open yet ..."

"Food bowl's empty," adds Velvet. "Belly's empty!"

I walk down to the kitchen. "Hey! I spy two bowls of cat food. You said your bowls were empty!"

"Food is stale," Velvet says. "Kibble is leftover." Ugh. Cats.

"You're up early for a Saturday," Mom says to me as she walks into the kitchen. She starts making coffee and checks her phone.

"Yeah, these guys wanted fresh food," I say.

Then my belly decides it has something to say. It's not shy about it either! *Rughhhhrrrr!*

We both hear it. She reads my mind.

"Ay, Marvellita, your stomach is asking for blueberry pancakes," Mom says.

"Blueberry pancakes always make my belly happy!" I say.

Mom takes out the pancake ingredients. Flour, sugar, milk, eggs, butter, blueberries, and vanilla.

"Today is a good day to start your report,"

Mom sneaks in.

I complain, "It's a *Saturday*. Plus, I don't even know what I'll write about."

"Isn't the answer clear, *mija*? Write about how habitat loss in El Yunque is harming the Boriquen parrot. Not enough people know it's a problem."

"How's my one little report gonna help?" I pout.

Mom dries her hands. "The more people know about it, the more help the parrots may get. Abuelita's getting older. To do more for the parrots, volunteers are needed. Donations, or money to help out, are needed."

"But isn't Abuelita a Speller, too? Can't she just do magic and fix the problem?" I ask.

"Yes, she is," Mom says. "But sometimes the natural world needs regular people, too. People all working together to solve big problems." She brings me my laptop.

"Ughhh," I say, "I guess ..."

"What do you mean you guess?" Mom says.

Her hands are on her hips. "Aren't you Marvelous Marvella? The magical Afro-Rican who talks to animals!"

"Maah-OM," I whine. "Its Saturdaaaay ..."

"Dear Marvelous Marvella," she says, as I do my bobblehead stare. "You made a wish. Were given a gift. Now you have a responsibility," Mom says. "Anyone can make a difference if they just try."

She pushes the laptop across the table.

"I just ... wish I was *there*," I say. "*In* Puerto Rico with Abuelita. I could talk to the animals there. Then I could help better. I can't do anything if I'm stuck in Buffalo! Can we just go there?"

"Well, that's not happening during a hurricane," Mom huffs. "So you do the next best thing. Help the parrots! Write!"

"Okay, okay ..." I say.

Tía Marisol walks in from the basement. That's where her mini-laboratory is. Her other laboratory is so much bigger—and cooler. That's where Mom took me after I got my Speller powers, to learn how to use them.

"Good morning," Tía says, holding a glass dish.

"Is that an experiment?" I ask.

Tía Marisol nods. "I'm trying to clone the unicorn berry plant," Tía says. "It's one of the Boriquen parrot's favorite magical foods. It always gives them strength after a big storm. But for the past few years, hurricanes have ruined every crop. And if there *are* any unicorn berries left in El Yunque, Abuelita has yet to find them."

"You make clones?" I ask, thinking about scary movies.

"I clone *plants*," Tía answers. "But every trial for the unicorn berries failed. I don't know what else to do."

"You *make* plants grow!" I say. That's the whole point of her power!

"Yes," Tía says. "But for some reason, this plant isn't listening."

Mom chimes in, "It might have to do with the hurricane. When Boriquen parrots are sick, hurt, or kidnapped from El Yunque, our powers can weaken."

Tía Marisol nods. "That was part of the *catch* you worried about, Marvellita."

Tía turns on the TV to see the weather. Dr. Angela Navarro is on. She's talking about

Hurricane Harley again. "The worst of Harley may be over soon in Puerto Rico," she says. "Experts on the island say that nearly 30 percent of the trees might be damaged, as well as tens of thousands of homes."

Mom's phone rings. She whispers to me, "It's Abuelita!" Into the phone, she says, "We just saw the news. It's pretty bad, isn't it? Are you okay?"

"My house is still standing," Abuelita says. "I am okay."

Mom sighs in relief. "What about the Boriquen parrot?"

"I can feel that they're out there somewhere—but I can't find them. We need to find them and give them some magical unicorn berries for strength. Without the unicorn berries, they may die out completely."

"And we will become regular people," Mom continues.

We all look at each other. I'm waiting for one of the adults to say something.

"I don't want to be a regular person again!" I say. What if I couldn't talk to my animal friends ever again?

"Don't worry, *mijita*," Abuelita says to me. But in her eyes, I can see she is worrying, too.

CHAPTER SEVEN

The Magical Dollhouse

I sit in my room, unsure of what to do. I don't want to write a *report* when I might be *losing my powers*. Then I hear Tip and Tap. Pudding and Velvet are running after them. *They* sound like a hurricane!

"Stop!" I yell. The mice stop running, then the cats. They all look at me. I usually don't yell at them so seriously. "Sorry, guys. I just don't know what to do." I tell them the whole story.

Tip says, "Maybe that dollhouse can help!"

"What dollhouse?" I say.

"In the secret room without the doorknob!"

"Show me!" I say. We go up to the attic.

Tip and Tap run under the door. Like they did before. But this time, a bright green light shines from beneath it. And all of a suddenly, the door opens.

The light is shining over a giant dollhouse in the room. It looks like a palace, big enough for me to crawl into. It's painted creamy white. A sky-blue door stands between four matching windows. I crawl through the door. There are four rooms decorated in fancy, royal-princess style.

Sitting on the floor of the first room is a toy coquí. It's got a big smile. The eyes seem to follow me. Then, I pick it up.

All of a suddenly, light, wind, and thunder blast around and over me! My whole entire body rushes, pushes, whizzes through a wind tunnel!

Just as suddenly, I'm jumping. I'm hopping through the forest! I'm surrounded by other coquís. Wait, a minute. What the ...? I've become a COQUÍ!?

"Hurry up!" the coquí says to me. "Don't wanna be tarantula food!"

"Tarantula!?" I shriek. "Where *are* we?"

We're jumping fast and high. Hundreds of us! "I am Carlos and this is El Yunque!"

We fly through tall grass. Over streams. Around canopies of trees and vines.

"Do you know where the Boriquen parrots are?"

"Of course!" says the coquí. "Follow me!"

I jump and jump, over green forest and trees that have been flattened by winds. I'm close to the parrots. I can feel it! I can hear them calling out. *Help us, help us ...*

The wind blows, lightning flashes, thunder cracks. I'm swooshing and swirling through another wind tunnel!

BAM!

CHAPTER EIGHT

Star Stories

I come to. Everything's all fuzzy. And everyone is yelling! "You said it wasn't activated!" Mom's yelling at Tía Marisol.

"It hasn't transported since before Marvella was born!" Tía argues. "Marvella made it work."

"It turned on all by itself!" I say defending myself. I sit up slowly.

"Marisol means your energy activated, or turned on, the dollhouse. Your power," Mom explains.

"You're what it's been waiting for all these years," Tía says. "A young Speller's energy."

"Did it take you to El Yunque when you

were little?" I ask.

"Yes!" Tía answers.

"Among other places," Mom says. "And times."

Telling them about my adventure, I see Tía is excited and Mom is worried.

"She has to return," Tía says. "The dollhouse will guide her. She needs to find the parrots."

"Marisol," Mom says to Tía. "She's not ready."

"She'll be ready, Monica," Tía says to Mom.

"Woah! Woah!" I exclaim. "What am I 'not ready' for?"

Mom is, well, scared. Mom's never scared.

"Let's make hot cocoa," Tía says.

Tía Marisol stirs the hot cocoa. Mom sprinkles a little chili pepper and cinnamon into the pot. "Sweet for your tongue. Hot for your hands. Spicy for your blood!" Mom says.

37

Sipping our cocoa, Tía and Mom tell me a story. About the dollhouse.

"Ophelia's brother, Rolando, made the dollhouse for her," Tía says. "Ophelia loved dolls. She made many. There are three still in the dollhouse.

Mom says, "Rolando used wood from trees grown on the edge of the crater made by the fallen star. The wood itself is magic."

"While he was building the dollhouse," Tía says, "Rolando's thoughts and dreams became part of the dollhouse's magic. He dreamed of traveling the world."

"Did Rolando travel in the dollhouse?" I ask.

"No," Tía says. "Only Spellers can use the power of the dollhouse. Ophelia used it to travel wherever she could to help with her powers."

"Today, you must use it to find and feed the Boriquen parrots," Tía says.

Yikes—that's more than I planned for a Saturday!

CHAPTER NINE

Three Roots Of The Same Tree

I crawl back into the dollhouse. This time I look around. The toy coquí is back in its dollhouse room. One room has a toy tower. One room is a ballroom. There are three dolls inside it.

One doll sits in a fancy gold chair. The body is made of white cotton fabric. Her black lace dress is long and puffy. Red silk is tied around her waist. Her face is shaded with black lace. Like a Spanish dancer!

A second doll stands beside a gold window. Her face is dark brown. She wears a belted long blue dress. The doll's tied headwrap is the same fabric as its belt. It reminds me of the women in photos Dad took when he was in Ghana, Africa, for a shoot.

The third doll wears a white dress. Her face is tan. She has two black braids. I get it! Spanish, West African, and Taíno! They're Boriqua dolls. The three parts that make us Puerto Rican. Mom told me that touching one of these dolls can take me to different times. Or places. What if I touch them all, together? Will that take me to Puerto Rico?

"One, two, three!" I shout before grabbing all three dolls.

Lightning flashes! Thunder rolls! Winds blow cold and warm! The floor opens, taking me away from here and now.

When I open my eyes, I'm lying in grass. The sky is blue. I see birds flying over my head, and I hear laughter.

"Wake up, Marvella!" a voice says. "We have somewhere to go!"

Three girls stand beside me. They look like the dolls!

"I am Yayo," says the Taíno girl.

"I am Angelita," says the Spanish girl.

"I am Akuba," says the West African girl. She hugs me.

"Akuba," Yayo says. "There isn't time. We

have to show her now!"

Walking through the forest, I hear the coquí voices. "KO-KEE KO-KEE!" Other animal voices are super loud here. I hear many more than I see. Yayo points to a few monkeys swinging above us!

"Ask them about the parrots," Yayo says. "You're the only one of us who can talk to them."

"Hello, monkeys," I say. "Have you seen the Boriquen parrots? They've been missing."

"They say to get closer to the mountain," I tell the other girls.

We walk further. Yayo leads the way. I see more fallen trees and hurricane damage. Walking beside me, Yayo says, "The forest protects us and feeds us. The trees here are all joined underground. Many roots. When we lose one, we lose a part of our family."

"We lose family when humans take our trees away," Akuba says.

"The hurricanes destroy trees, too," I say.

"But nature always repairs its damage," Angelica adds. "Humans need to help, too."

Reaching the mountain, I see a parrot in a tree. "We must be here," I say, pointing to the parrot before it flies away.

The mountain blocks us from walking further. Akuba motions to us. "Look," she says. "A cave!"

We walk deeper into the cave. It's so dark! No parrot would want to live here! Then, I see a light. We walk out of the cave and into a magical place with waterfalls, green plants, and lots of flowers. A place untouched by the hurricane.

"Unicorn berries!" I say, pointing to bushes full of the magical fruit. "But they're so far away from the parrots that need them. I need to bring my Tía Marisol here. She'll know what to do! How can I get here in real life?"

Yayo says, "When magic fails, love will find a way."

And just like that, they're gone! And so am I, tumbling out of the dollhouse.

42

CHAPTER TEN

Finding A Way

Mom and Tía are excited about the cave adventure. Mom makes me potato and cheese *pastelillos,* or turnovers. I'm *really* hungry. "Now I know where the parrots are hiding after the hurricane!" I say.

"But we still have a puzzle," Tía Marisol says. "How does Abuelita find the cave?"

"If I was in El Yunque," I say, "I know I could find it."

"That's the big problem, Marvellita," Mom says. "You're not in El Yunque. Buffalo is far from Puerto Rico. It's even harder to get there after a hurricane."

I frown. All of a suddenly, I get an idea!

43

"Yayo said that when magic fails, love will find a way. And Mom, *you* said that my report could make people care about the animals that need help. So, we need to find a way to make a whole lot of people care!"

"How will we do that, Marvellita?" Mom says, looking at me in wonder. I like when she listens to my ideas.

I say, "When disasters happen, people always help. I see it on TV all the time. Hurricanes, fires, floods, earthquakes! Even snowstorms here in Buffalo. When bad stuff happens, people care enough to help each other. Abuelita is always saying we need 'more hands.' We need more hearts, too."

"But how?" Tía Marisol asks.

"Tía, you said that you know Dr. Angela Navarro from the weather channel. Millions of people watch her show! If she talks about what's going on, people will listen."

Tía Marisol's eyes light up. "What a great idea, Marvellita! I have a call to make."

She talks on the phone for a long time. Mom makes me more food. Then Tía walks in the room. "Great news! Dr. Angela wants to do a special report on the hurricane and the Boriquen parrots."

"A report like my homework?" I ask.

"No, a *big* news story!" laughs Tía Marisol. "And it gets better. The crew flies to Puerto Rico tomorrow on a special plane. The plane has three empty seats. Wanna help the Boriquen parrots?"

There's nothing else I'd rather do!

CHAPTER ELEVEN

At Home in Boriquen

When the airplane lands in Puerto Rico, Mom and Tía seem like they've just come home. They also seem really sad when they see all the damage from Hurricane Harley. We drive to El Yunque in silence. It's hard to imagine the cooling breeze can also become a dangerous wind.

We meet Abuelita outside the forest, talking to a lot of people. Dr. Angela is there. Other people stand by. I run up to Abuelita and hug her so tight. "Oh Marvellita, I'm so proud of you."

Tía Marisol is talking to Dr. Angela. "My friend Magaly teaches at the University of

Puerto Rico," Dr. Angela says to us. "I asked if she could get some volunteers!"

"Do we have enough hands to search for and find our parrots?" I ask Abuelita.

"Sí, *mijita*!" she answers. "I believe we do!"

The volunteers begin clearing fallen trees and branches. "During storms, parrots and other birds hide under shrubs," Abuelita tells us.

While they search for lost birds, Tía Marisol, Abuelita, and I search for the unicorn berry oasis.

When I doubt my direction, Tía Marisol reminds me to ask for help. "If we're lost, ask the animals," she says. "We can't succeed on our own."

The monkeys and coquís help guide me to the cave. The animals know and see things humans miss. Being a Speller means I must work with animals. I must do good and use my magic to help. Even if that means working on a weekend or my winter break!

The monkeys lead us to the mountain cave entrance. It's hidden by broken branches.

But the monkeys see it's only camouflage. Together we find an opening. We walk through the dark, dark cave. Then, we reach the magical land.

"An oasis!" says Abuelita. "A perfect, untouched place."

There are even more unicorn berry bushes than in my dollhouse travels. Hummingbirds and butterflies fly around.

Abuelita walks to a waterfall and opens her arms. I can feel her magic grow strong! She can feel the forest. "Marvellita," she says. "The parrots are near. Tell them to come closer. Only *you* can speak to them."

"Nothing to be afraid of!" I shout to the parrots. "Lots of unicorn berries to eat. Come on home!"

All of a suddenly, Boriquen parrots appear from the sky. They rest on Abuelita's arms. One lands on my shoulder. We follow Abuelita and feed them unicorn berries. I see their wings glitter with magic. They share their sparkle with us, too!

Tía Marisol touches a unicorn berry bush and it grows even bigger. "My powers are back up and running!"

Abuelita kisses my cheek. "You made a big difference today, Marvellita."

"And I didn't even need to write my report for school!" I say.

Tía says, "You still have to write the
report, Marvella. You just have more to write
about."

I roll my eyes. But then a parrot lands on
my shoulder. "We can't tell Dr. Angela about the
magic, right?"

Tía Marisol shakes her head. "No, but even without the magic, people will care about these animals. They will volunteer to help this habitat and give money to keep it safe. Love will find a way."

"Go on and find the camera crew, parrots!" I tell them. "Let them see you."

The Boriquen parrots fly up and up through the trees and into the light.

Want to Keep Reading?

If you liked this book, check out another book
from a West 44 Books series.

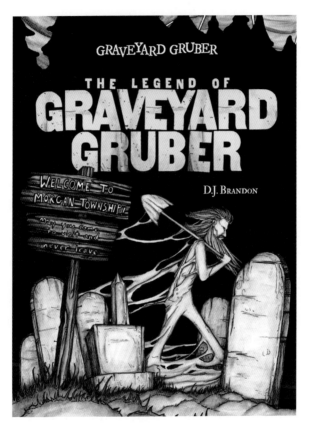

9781538384930

ONE
THE CHALLENGE

The brown and white sign said, "*Welcome to Morgan Township! May you come to visit and never leave.*"

Never leave? It seemed like a creepy message. I mean, it was right across the road from a cemetery. And it was the biggest cemetery any of us had ever seen.

But that cemetery was about to put an end to my totally uncool name, Grady Gruber. Who would put *that* on a kid's birth certificate? It had haunted me my whole eight years.

"Quick, hold your breath!" Ruby said.

Ruby is my little sister. And I had taught her that. All the kids know. You have to hold your breath when you pass a cemetery. That's so the ghosts can't steal your spirit!

It had been a long drive to Morgan Township for our Bose County baseball game, past a whole lot of stinky cow pastures and windmills and stuff. The cemetery was the most excitement we'd had.

So, quick as lightning, we all gulped great big breaths—and held them!

Ruby only lasted five seconds. Then Little Jake crumbled. His breath burst all over the back seat.

"I had to," he panted. "My brains were going to explode!"

Lindy was next. She's an awesome ball player. She was named after Lindy McDaniel, of the St. Louis Cardinals. Breath-holding, though, was not her thing. "Can't do it," she said. She slouched back in the seat, gasping.

Dez and I were the only ones left. Just me and the coolest kid in the whole third grade! Our eyes locked.

It wasn't enough that Dez was our lead pitcher. Or that he had the coolest hair ever. Or that his dad was the Town of Evans fire chief!

No, I thought. *It's my turn. I'm gonna outlast*

Dez. And I'm gonna make it all the way to the end of the cemetery!

But the cemetery went on forever! My face was getting warm.

What was I thinking? No one beats The Dez.

Even his eyes were cool. As cool as steel. My chest felt heavy.

I can't give in to him. It's my turn!

The van was crawling past the cemetery.

Dez's face was getting redder and redder. We were staring each other down, each waiting for the explosion of air.

And then, it came!

"BAHHHH!" Dez's breath blasted out! And suddenly, everyone was looking at me!

I felt my eyes bulging as I watched out the window.

Oh, no!

Mom had slowed the van for a couple of cows that were swaying across the road.

The car inched forward.

Only three more rows of gravestones! My brain felt all fuzzy and weird.

"He looks really funny," I heard Lindy say. Her voice sounded far away.

"Yeah," Little Jake echoed.

Dez leaned forward to get a look at me. His face seemed strange. It was all wobbly. And his neck looked like a giraffe's! What was happening to me?

Then, like a foghorn, Ruby's voice, all urgent: "Mom! Something's wrong with Grady!"

about the author

Annette Daniels Taylor loves cats, butterflies, babies, dogs, books, dreaming, and plants. She has so many plants inside her Buffalo home she stopped counting at 300! Her favorites are Rhipsalis, Peperomia, Orchids, Philodendron, Pothos, Hoya, and well, most plants that trail, hang, and just grow. Annette is from Staten Island, New York, and she got married and started a family in Brooklyn. One day, after her husband got sick, they packed up and moved to his hometown of Buffalo. Like Marvella, Annette misses Brooklyn, but now Buffalo is home.

OTHER TITLES IN THIS SERIES:

MARVELLA FINDS HER MAGIC
MARVELLA IS A MODEL

Check out more books at:
www.west44books.com

An imprint of Enslow Publishing

WEST **44** BOOKS™